Henry Holt and Company, LLC, *Publishers since 1866*
115 West 18th Street, New York, New York 10011

Henry Holt is a registered trademark of Henry Holt and Company, LLC

First published in the United States in 2001 by Henry Holt and Company, LLC.
Originally published in the United Kingdom in 2000 by Andersen Press Ltd.

Library of Congress Cataloging-in-Publication Data
Foreman, Michael.
Cat in the manger / Michael Foreman.
Summary: A small cat reminisces about events that took place around
the manger where it was sleeping on the night the baby Jesus was born.
[1. Jesus Christ—Nativity—Juvenile fiction. 2. Jesus Christ—Nativity—Fiction.
3. Cats—Fiction. 4. Domestic animals—Fiction. 5. Christmas—Fiction.] I. Title.
PZ7.F7583 Cav 2001 [E]—dc21 00-47300

ISBN 0-8050-6677-2
First American Edition—2001
Printed in Italy on acid-free paper. ∞

1 3 5 7 9 10 8 6 4 2

Cat in the Manger

MICHAEL ✦ FOREMAN

HENRY HOLT AND COMPANY

NEW YORK

It was really cold that night, I remember. A dusting of snow and bright, bright stars, so I was glad the cows were there to keep me warm.

But just as the barn was getting nice and warm, the door flew open, and there stood a man and a woman astride a donkey in a flurry of snowflakes.

The donkey looked meek and mild, but I kept out of his way, just in case.

The man pulled some fresh straw down from the loft and made a bed for the woman in the corner farthest from the door. She looked uncomfortable. When she cried out, the man embraced her, and the donkey went dewy-eyed.

Then I heard a baby cry.

The cows and the goats were all wide awake now, shuffling about and treading on each other's toes. Unceremoniously, I was tipped out of the manger!

The baby stopped crying. Every-thing was silent. It was as if all the animals held their breath. We looked at the baby, and the baby looked at us.

Suddenly I heard sheep. Bleating sheep. I could hear them coming closer and closer. Then, with an icy blast, the door flew open and in stumbled some shepherds and snow-covered sheep.

The shepherds knelt on the mud floor around the man and the woman and smiled at the baby.

Then came the camels. There were three of them.

The camels were enormous. Their red-and-green leather bridles sparkled with gold decorations. Their three masters were clad even more magnificently.

They looked like kings, yet they knelt down beside the shepherds and all the animals in the barn, and smiled at the baby.

Above, chickens sat silent in the rafters. When I looked behind me, I saw rows and rows of mice.

Mice! Their beady little eyes flickered from me to the baby and back again.

Just you wait! I turned my gaze back to the baby.

The mice crept forward, passed me, and scampered through to the front . . . all eyes on the baby.

It all seems like a long time ago now. Everyone is gone. The shepherds with their bleating sheep, the rich men with their grumpy camels. Even the man and the woman with the baby are gone.

The funny thing is, I haven't caught a mouse since. I chase them occasionally, just for practice, but I haven't the heart to catch one.